THE GOVERNESS
A PROFESSOR CHALLENGER STORY

Works by the Same Author

NIGHTMARE, WITH ANGEL
Crown 8vo, cloth, 9s.
PRESENTATION EDITION 10s. 6d. net

DOWN RIVER
Cloth, 7s. net

RAIN
Cloth, 7s. net

THE BOAT HOUSE
Cloth, 7s. net

THE SPIRIT BOX
Cloth, 7s. net

LONDON: THE BROOLIGAN PRESS

Our union was broken there and then, in the sitting-room of Folkestone's Imperial Hotel, never to be restored.

THE GOVERNESS
Stephen Gallagher

THE BROOLIGAN PRESS
LONDON
NEW YORK

This story is a work of fiction. Certain names, characters, places, and incidents either are the product of the author's imagination or are used fictitiously. Any resemblance to actual persons, living or dead, events, or locales is entirely coincidental

This edition published 2021 by The Brooligan Press
Rights and Permissions: Howard Morhaim Literary Agency
30 Pierrepont St, Brooklyn NY 11201

Stephen Gallagher has asserted his right to be identified as the author of this Work in accordance with the Copyright, Designs and Patents Act 1988

All rights reserved. No part of this publication may be reproduced, stored in a retrieval system, or transmitted in any form or by any means, electronic, mechanical, photocopying, recording or otherwise, without the prior permission of the copyright owner

Illustration by Walter S Stacey

Copyright © 2021 Stephen Gallagher

ISBN: 978 1 9160578 5 2

*And some in dreams assurèd were
Of the Spirit that plagued us so;
Nine fathom deep he had followed us
From the land of mist and snow.*

*The Rime of the Ancient Mariner
(text of 1834)
Samuel Taylor Coleridge*

up the silver in his beard which, unlike the days of old, he now wore trimmed. I could only imagine that Enid had persuaded him to a concession that her mother had never managed. Perhaps time and grief had done their work, but the Wild Man of Science seemed relatively dapper and almost subdued.

An hour of hymns and speeches was followed by a much livelier hour of clairvoyance, reaching its height with the manifestation of the deceased author in the empty chair beside his widow. That is, if the medium were to be believed, which few saw any reason to doubt. When the meeting ended and the excited crowd moved as one into the streets, I fought the tide to reach the carriage entrance before Challenger's motor car. I got there just as it arrived to collect him. When his driver returned to the wheel, I jumped in from the other side.

"Sir," I began, "I know I'm unwelcome here. But please—" And that was as far as it went, because the Professor had me by the collar and was flinging open the door to throw me headfirst into the street.

I said quickly, "Hear me out and I'll agree to the divorce."

His grip didn't lessen, but he stayed his hand.

He said, "You dare to offer terms?"

"No terms," I said. "I'll take whatever conditions you name."

I was released. As I eased my collar and dropped back onto the seat the Professor commanded, "Once around the park, Austin." And then, to me: "I don't want Enid getting sight of you."

"I appreciate this, sir."

"Save your appreciation. Say your piece and then get out."

"Do you recall the children at Chorley Grange?"

Those fierce eyes narrowed, and I had his attention.

"I do," he said. "What of them?"

Chorley Grange was a burned-out manor house where the four of us—Challenger, his daughter

Perhaps time and grief had done their work, but the Wild Man of Science seemed relatively dapper and almost subdued.

Enid, the medium Algernon Mailey, and myself—had once responded to reports of a juvenile haunting. It had begun as a whispering in the ruins, followed by sightings of movement through the window of the former nursery. Someone appeared to be inside, yet the room always proved to be empty. We spirit-hunters set up camp, with Challenger and Mailey at the house while Enid and I looked into its history. Enid reported 'powerful vibrations' from three unmarked graves in the nearby churchyard, while Mailey contacted the spirits of those who'd died in the fire. Ghosts and graves proved to be connected. They were children who had strayed from the *limbus infantium* through which they were meant to pass, and did not know how to return.

A common occurrence with children who predecease their parents, according to Mailey. With no one to shepherd them, they wander; and having lost their way, can only cling to the familiar.

I said to Challenger, "I've been visited by the boy."

I didn't need to say which.

"You mean the *b*—," he said.

"I mean my son."

"And you dare speak of this to me."

"You've agreed to listen."

"My tolerance has its limits," he said, and then, to his driver, to call our meeting to an end, "Austin!"

"The boy is dead," I said.

There was a long silence. The driver awaited instruction which did not come.

Challenger said, "Go on."

"I saw him first at the end of my street, then three nights later at my window."

"This was when?"

"Last week. When I went out, he was gone. I took it as a sign of trouble and sought out the mother. She confessed that the boy died last winter. She'd kept silent in order to continue receiving the money."

"You can't expect honesty from a blackmailer."

"There was no blackmail. I paid willingly. But

through my solicitor—there had been no contact between us since the child's birth. I refused to see him, but I had enquiries made. At the time it seemed for the best."

"Then how could you know him now?"

"I knew him," I said.

The child had been the outcome of a pre-matrimonial experience. This was the substance of the confession I'd made to Enid when, swept up in our newlywed bliss, we had sworn to a shared life with no secrets between us. Our union was broken there and then, in the sitting-room of Folkestone's Imperial Hotel, never to be restored.

At that time the child was three years old. The mother was a woman I had barely known. In the past week I'd learned that she had taken the role of a widow and raised the boy alone. Their life had been difficult. He had died a charity case, I was told, in the Evelina Hospital for Sick Children.

"He's lost, George," I said. "A lost soul. We helped the Chorley Grange children to peace. He deserves no less. Blame me as the sole author of

Enid's pain, George, but the boy is an innocent."

For all his ire, bluster, and ego, I knew that Challenger was a decent man. I saw that I had reached him when he let my slip into familiarity pass. He had the reputation of one who did not suffer fools gladly, which was an understatement. He suffered nobody gladly. He looked out of the window for a while, thinking. The park outside lay silent under the light of the quarter moon.

He said, "Mailey has passed beyond."

"I know," I said. Our late colleague had used his powers to engineer the delivery of the Chorley Grange children to some higher care.

"With Mailey gone we need some other way," the Professor said.

He leaned forward and gave his driver an address in Bloomsbury, whereupon the motor vehicle turned from the park and we headed East along the Bayswater Road.

We visited three different houses, finding no reply at the first and only a maid to answer at each of the others. At the last of them, in Bedford Square, Challenger sought the use of a telephone and returned to the vehicle after ten minutes. His expression was dark. On this night, perhaps the most significant of the Spiritualists' year, it seemed there wasn't a single reputable psychic of his acquaintance who'd stayed at home.

I dared not suggest that we might call upon Enid for help.

I asked what joy, and he ignored me. "To Ralston Street," Challenger told his driver. "Number One."

When we arrived at the Chelsea address, he told me to wait in the car. I recognised the house, a tall narrow building with railings around the basement and seven steps up to the door. It was here that Miss Gwendoline Otter held her regular salons, attended mostly by young actresses and literary figures. I wondered at the point of our visit until Challenger emerged a few minutes later, followed by a jowly, balding man of fifty-something years in a shapeless brown suit and floppy bow tie. Though I recognised the man I wasn't sure of his name, because he had several; I knew only that he preferred to be known as La Paix.

I moved over as he made for the seat beside me. He landed heavily, looked me over and then said to Challenger, "Is this him?" There was nothing of the French about his accent, unless I'd missed the news of France annexing Warwickshire.

"Tell him your tale, Malone," Challenger said. I couldn't say if the distaste in his manner was for my story, or for our new companion.

As we headed for our guest's Paddington apartments, I went over it again. When I was done, La Paix turned to Challenger and said, "Took something for you to come to me, George. What do I get out of this?"

"You get the satisfaction of hearing me ask," Challenger said.

La Paix settled back into the limousine's upholstery.

"Worth it," he said happily.

We ascended to La Paix's flat, to be met by a

startled and nervous male companion who seemed to be part-dependent, part-housekeeper, part-something I couldn't define. The two men left us alone and for a few seconds I could hear furious whispering in the next room. The chamber we were in was run-down, dark, and unsettling, with a round wooden dining table and half a dozen chairs. Soot had blackened the ceiling above the table, and damp had stained the walls.

The companion reappeared and, with ill grace and a foul expression, spread a circular cloth on the table. The cloth was decorated with various occult symbols. In the centre of it he banged down a bowl containing dried weeds which, after several attempts, he managed to set to smouldering.

La Paix then rejoined us. He'd changed his clothes and was now barelegged in a dressing gown that I think was meant to be some kind of ceremonial robe. The companion made a noisy departure to the kitchen and the three of us sat around the table, forming three points of a triangle.

"Breathe deep of the incense," La Paix said.

"It's essential to the ceremony."

Stove heat had already made the air in the room close and oppressive, and at the very first whiff of incense my head began to ache. This was no séance. Or at least, it resembled none that I'd ever attended. Unable to locate a psychic, Challenger had been forced to resort to a mystic. La Paix produced a tattered scroll from his sleeve and read from it, and then he made an incantation. All of this in a language that might, for all I know, have been of his own invention.

Then he asked me, "The boy's name?"

And I had to admit, "I don't know."

"I need to locate his vibrations in the ether. For that I will require certain information. Tell me about the mother. Was she pretty?"

"In honesty? No."

"The truth."

I had no escape. I was painfully aware that I was speaking in the presence of my estranged father-in-law.

I confessed, "She appealed. In the moment."

"The moment is where we begin," La Paix then said.

What followed was an interrogation on matters of such intimate detail that I'm convinced the questions were more for La Paix' private gratification than for the gathering of any useful facts. I grew more embarrassed. Challenger grew increasingly angry, and rose to leave.

"It's essential that you stay, Professor," La Paix said mildly. And then he leaned forward and fanned the incense smoke toward himself with both hands, inhaling deeply.

Then he sat back with his eyes closed.

"The boy follows you," he said. "He's close to you. But as you've denied him, he can never come near."

I said, "Tell me what to do."

"Find the Governess, and place him in her care."

There was a puzzled silence from both of us, and then Challenger said, "The Governess?"

"The entity charged with the care of young

souls in limbo," La Paix explained. "Not a job you would envy. Those souls are legion. Their noise is deafening. And they never stay put."

"Good Lord," Challenger said.

And I said, "How do we find her?"

La Paix bent forward again and took another deep draught of the fumes, so deep that he couldn't catch his breath and went into a coughing fit. We waited until he'd done spluttering. Then he wiped his eyes and composed himself.

"I see another boy. Atop a rock or a broken tree. Spirits and creatures swirl around it. He blows a pipe."

I recognised the description immediately. "The Pan statue," I said. "Peter Pan. The bronze in Kensington Gardens."

"I was getting to that," La Paix said, irritated. "It draws those young souls entranced by it in life. The Governess knows the place well. It's one of her regular collection points."

Challenger said, "Will we find her there?"

"If you hurry," La Paix said. He dug in the

pockets of his robe, and brought out something that he slid across the table. "Show her this. It will tell her you came from me."

I expected some kind of personal token, but it was a coin. A foreign coin, one of those odd ones with a hole in the middle. I picked it up and saw that it was an ordinary ten-centime piece.

Challenger said, "Why should she care who sent us?"

"She's the Governess," La Paix said. "She has a duty to the lost. This creates a debt that I can someday call upon."

The Professor's patience had now worn thin. He pushed his chair back and said, "Are we done? I'll have Austin bring the car."

"No," La Paix said. "Walk."

So we walked, from Praed Street to Kensington Gardens, through empty streets and into the park, with Challenger's man in the Daimler following at a distance. It was a mile or less. When street lighting fell behind us, the vehicle's lamps helped to show the way.

Every now and again, I would look back. If I turned quickly enough, I'd catch the silhouette of a small figure in the corner of my eye. I was in no doubt that it was a genuine presence. Yet whenever I tried to bring him fully into focus, he'd be gone.

Challenger said, "Is he with us?"

"He is," I said.

Among the things I'd learned in my confrontation with the boy's mother; she'd told him that his father had been a soldier, an officer, a hero who had died in some foreign war that was never specified. She supported the fiction with two medals bought from a pawnbrokers'. These had become the boy's proudest possessions, kept in a tin box under his bed.

We were well into the park now. Down the path by the Long Water we could see our way to the clearing around the statue. Pale stone around the base, a gleam of polished bronze above. There seemed to be movement around it, but when we reached the spot there was no one.

We stood there, looking around. I was about to express my disappointment when Challenger said, "I hear them. Don't you?"

"Who?"

"Children. I hear children's voices." And before I could respond, he'd raced off into the dark. I tried to follow, but I'd already lost him.

Then I heard him—or someone—crashing around in another part of the undergrowth. Then a silence; and then, somewhere in the near distance, a soft whistle.

"You heard that, I hope," the Professor said close to my ear.

I turned and found him behind me. He quickly raised a finger to his lips for silence and beckoned me to follow.

"See," he whispered.

The fresh air had done little to clear my head after the poisonous fug of the mystic's lounge, and now I began to doubt my senses. I knew Kensington Gardens as a park of broad walks and wide open spaces, but it was as if we'd struck out from the statue in a direction with no counterpart on any map.

As we pressed onward the shrubbery grew ever denser, the pathways more confined. Our way was crossed by a broad grove, of the kind you'd expect to lead to a garden temple or other such feature.

At the far end of the grove, I saw children. Spectral children, a dozen or more of them, small and shining with a faint light all of their own. And at the centre of the group, towering above them, a dark figure that gave no light at all; but rather absorbed it, drawing it in, creating a centre of night around which those little planets revolved. This swirling group was there for a moment, and then it moved from the end and out of our sight.

"Quickly," Challenger said, and as he moved I followed.

We reached the turn. The temperature seemed to fall where the paths met. The last traces of a moving glow drew us on to the next juncture. And then again and again, turn after turn, with Challenger setting a pace.

"Wait," I said, but he wouldn't wait. My head spun. I looked up and saw no clouds, no quarter moon, no stars. Yet there was light enough to see by, as if we now moved in a luminous mist.

And then, as I lowered my gaze to look back, there he was. Not the Professor, but the boy, fully disclosed to my sight and closer than ever.

I turned to tell Challenger, and saw snow. Falling snowflakes, in July. And the foliage around us crusted with ice. I looked for the boy again.

"It's working," Challenger said. "He's being drawn in with the others."

"Professor, I'm confused," I said. "I don't know where we are."

"You're right to be," he said. "I believe we stand on the threshold of the *limbus infantium*."

And then I heard a woman's voice behind us, saying, "Go back, gentlemen. There's nothing for you here."

The dark veil mostly shadowed her face. I think she was young. It's impossible to say. The

I SAID, "MIGHT YOU BE THE GOVERNESS?"

snowflakes fell around her head and shoulders. Instead of settling they seemed to pass on through.

"Now, Malone," Challenger said in a low voice. "Remember what you came for."

My legs were unsteady but I felt Challenger's strong grip on my shoulder, and I was able to find words.

I said, "Might you be the Governess?"

She made no move to reply but then I was distracted for a moment, as another stream of young figures flickered right by me. I had my answer. They were like children called home for supper. Except that they were only briefly substantial, barely on the edge of existence, and I thought I saw the boy among them.

"Now go," she said. "Return. Before you forget the way."

But there was business to transact before we could leave. I reached into my pocket for the ten-centime piece and held it out.

"Here," I said. She looked at the coin. She made no move to take it.

"We brought you a soul," I said. "This is a token so you'll remember the debt."

She sighed, then. Not the reaction I'd expected.

"Don't tell me," she said. "La Paix."

"You're acquainted?"

"Far too well."

She moved on without taking the coin. I wasn't sure what to do next. But Challenger was there by her side, moving with her, the scientist in him compelled to seize this unique opportunity.

"You seem weary," he said. "Why?"

"For the children this is place of passage," she said. "For me it's hell. The innocent will eventually move on. I never will."

"Why not?"

"For a sin I can no longer remember. Bound by my duty, and now at the beck of the likes of La Paix." She almost spat his name with bitterness, and I began to imagine being a trapped soul condemned to be at a disadvantage to any low wretch who could mangle a spell.

We reached a clearing then. But what a clearing.

Here the children were waiting. Imagine a field of a billion young souls, their faces turned toward us, a vast army, on and on until their outer numbers were lost to view. My very breath stopped in my body at the overwhelming sight.

The Governess paused and looked at me, as if an idea had occurred to her.

"Let me discharge the debt, and owe La Paix nothing," she said. "Take back your boy."

I failed to understand. "Take him where?" I said.

"To life," she said.

But Challenger said, "Take him back into life? Can that be done?"

"I don't see why not," she said. "I can hardly be damned for it."

She held out her hand. I placed the coin in her cold palm.

"It's done," she said. Then she smiled. "But only if you can find him. And dawn approaches. The door between the worlds is closing as we speak."

The Governess

A trick. I'd fallen for a trick. I looked back toward that endless gathering, a single night's work for the Governess. How could I ever hope to find one half-glimpsed face among so many?

But the Professor strode forward, and with all the power and force of the old Challenger that I remembered so well, bellowed, "Which of you is this man's child? Cry out and take your place back in the world!"

I was hit as if by a blast as a billion yearning voices answered him. I clapped my hands over my ears, but Challenger stood firm before the in-rushing tide of sound. I was overwhelmed, I had no chance… but the Professor knew what he was doing.

"There," he said. "Tell me I'm wrong."

And with the noise still raging, I followed his pointing finger to the one child who stood, mute and silent amongst all the others, with his accusing eyes upon me.

The roar subsided. The Governess shrugged.

"Fair enough," she said. "Now I suggest you go

back while you still can."

"And the bargain?" Challenger said.

"Will be honoured," she said.

We emerged in West Norwood. Do not ask me how. With no way of getting a message to Challenger's driver, we walked to Gipsy Hill Station for a train on the Crystal Palace line.

Challenger said, "I'll have the divorce papers delivered for your signature."

I'd completely forgotten my promise. But a deal is a deal.

I said, "Please tell Enid I wish her well."

That, it seemed, was expecting too much. But I could not complain. I'd been given the help that I'd sought, and we'd found a resolution of a kind. Though what form that resolution would take, I had yet to discover.

It was grey dawn when I reached my lodgings on Gower Street. I threw my coat on a chair and prised off my boots and dropped onto the bed, exhausted. Though my body was spent, my mind spun like a dynamo. I had acted, but I had no idea what would happen now.

As the events of the last few hours moved from the immediacy of experience into the memory of it, I began to examine the evening's narrative as a third party might, and to interrogate it with a journalist's eye. Just how much of the story could I 'stand up' from the moment we'd settled around that filthy table in that incense-choked room? La Paix was a known self-promoter and charlatan. He couldn't be compared to a reputable psychic like Algernon Mailey. In his daily life, Mailey had been a barrister and family man. La Paix flirted with the occult, and his powers were rooted in narcotics and depravity.

The longer I spent fending off sleep and reviewing my thoughts, the more that last night took on the character of an opium dream.

And yet.

And yet, if it could only be.

I thought of the boy with his medals in a tin box, worshipping a father who lived only in his imagination. A man next to whom I cut a much diminished, far less admirable figure.

No wonder we are seduced so easily by fantasies of second chances, by the dream of turning back time. Once I'd had a career, and once Enid had loved me. But now I was finding that the greater torment drew its power from a charity bed in the Evelina Hospital for Sick Children.

By now the city's birds had begun their chorus and I was no closer to sleep. I'd run out of new thoughts and my mind was just rehearsing the same themes, over and over. It was at this point that a tentative knock came at my door.

I froze. I listened.

The rest of the house was silent. And then, just as I was becoming convinced that I'd imagined it, the sound came again.

Someone knocking, for sure.

A light rap, as if by a small fist, tapping with a coin against the wood.

A LIGHT RAP, AS IF BY A SMALL FIST, TAPPING WITH A COIN AGAINST THE WOOD.

TALES FEATURING SEBASTIAN BECKER
THE SPECIAL INVESTIGATOR TO THE LORD CHANCELLOR'S VISITOR IN LUNACY

By
STEPHEN GALLAGHER
AUTHOR OF "VALLEY OF LIGHTS," "THE BOAT HOUSE," "THE SPIRIT BOX," ETC.

Chancery lunatics were people of wealth or property whose fortunes were at risk from their madness. Those deemed unfit to manage their affairs saw them taken over by lawyers of the Crown, known as the Masters of Lunacy. It was Sebastian's employer, the Lord Chancellor's Visitor, who would decide their fate. Though the office was intended to be a benevolent one, many saw him as an enemy to be outwitted or deceived, even to the extent of concealing criminal insanity.

It was for such cases that the Visitor had engaged Sebastian. His job was to seek out the cunning dissembler, the dangerous madman whose resources might otherwise make him untouchable. Rank and the social order gave such people protection. A former British police detective and one-time Pinkerton man, Sebastian had been engaged to work 'off the books' in exposing their misdeeds. His modest salary was paid out of the department's budget. He remained a shadowy figure, an investigator with no public profile.

THE KINGDOM OF BONES

When prizefighter-turned-stage manager Tom Sayers is wrongly accused in the slayings of pauper children, he disappears into a twilight world of music halls and temporary boxing booths. While Sayers pursues the elusive actress Louise Porter, the tireless Detective Inspector Sebastian Becker is on his trail.

THE BEDLAM DETECTIVE

An inventor and industrialist made rich by his weapons patents, Sir Owain Lancaster is haunted by the tragic outcome of an ill-judged Amazon expedition in which his entire party was killed. When local women are found slain on his land, he claims that the same dark Lost-World forces have followed him home.

THE AUTHENTIC WILLIAM JAMES

Sebastian Becker delivers justice to those dangerous madmen whose fortunes might otherwise place them above the law. But in William James he faces a different challenge; to prove a man sane, so that he may hang. Did the reluctant showman really burn down a crowded pavilion with the audience inside? And if not, why is this British sideshow cowboy so determined to shoulder the blame?

Printed in Great Britain
by Amazon